go girl

Flower
Girl

hardie grant EGMONT

Flower Girl
first published in 2008
this edition published in 2011 by
Hardie Grant Egmont
Ground Floor, Building 1, 658 Church Street
Richmond, Victoria 3121, Australia
www.hardiegrantegmont.com.au

A CiP record for this title is available from the National Library of Australia

Text copyright © 2008 Chrissie Perry
Illustration and design copyright © 2011 Hardie Grant Egmont

Illustration by Aki Fukuoka
Design by Michelle Mackintosh
Text design and typesetting by Ektavo

Printed in Australia by Griffin Press, an Accredited ISO AS/NZS
14001:2004 Environmental Management System printer.

3 5 7 9 10 8 6 4

Flower Girl

by
Chrissie Perry

Illustrations by
Aki Fukuoka

hardie grant EGMONT

Chapter One

'Hold still, Lola! If you keep wriggling around like that, Katya won't be able to get your proper measurements.'

Lola giggled. 'But it *tickles*, Mum,' she said. Her mum grinned back as Katya wrapped the tape measure around Lola's waist. Lola's eyes scanned the room.

A big rack in the corner held lots of

long dresses. Lola thought they all looked beautiful. She could see a dress with a frill that flicked out, almost touching the ground. If she crouched down from the stool she was standing on, she could see the sequins on the neckline of a powder blue dress on the end of the rack. They glittered like a thousand tiny stars, as though someone had pulled them out of the sky and sewn them on …

'Lola, can you stand straight and tall for Katya?' Lola's mum asked.

'If I measure you while you're bobbing down like that, we'll end up with a mini-dress,' said Katya.

'Oops, sorry,' Lola said, straightening

up so that Katya could measure the length from her waist to her knees.

'So, let's see,' Katya said with a smile, glancing down at the picture that Lola and her mum had drawn together. 'I think I may have the perfect fabric for this dress. Wait here for a minute.'

As Katya ducked into the back room, Lola jumped down from the little stool and bumped, *smack*, into something.

The *something* she'd bumped into was a dressmaker's dummy.

'Oh, hello Headless,' she joked.

There were three dressmaker's dummies scattered around the room. They had no heads, and where their legs should have been was a pole on a stand.

Two of the dummies wore half-finished

dresses, but the one Lola bumped into was completely undressed, except for a thousand pins with pearl tips sticking into her.

'Ouch, you poor thing,' Lola laughed, nodding at Headless. 'But don't you think you should put some clothes on?'

'Headless is going to help me with a wedding gown this afternoon,' explained Katya. She stood at the door with her hands behind her back. 'So, ladies,' said Katya. 'Are you ready to see what I found? It's pretty special.'

Lola clasped both hands together when she saw what Katya was holding.

'Oh, it's … it's …' Lola searched for the right word. Beautiful? Lovely? No word seemed quite good enough to describe the fabric Katya was holding out.

It was Lola's favourite colour in the whole world. Purple! The exact type of purple Lola had dreamt her dress would be. Not a mushy mauve, but something deeper and stronger ... like a violet. As Katya pulled the material from the giant roll, Lola reached out to touch it. It was soft and smooth.

'So, do you think this is OK?' Katya asked.

Lola sighed dreamily. 'It's *perfect*,' she said.

'Good,' Katya replied, picking up the drawing Lola and her mum had drawn.

'When you come back in two weeks, I'll have your dress ready for a fitting. Then, you can pick it up the week after that.'

Lola screwed up her nose. Three weeks seemed a very long time to wait for her dress. She'd imagined herself walking out of the dressmaker's with a beautiful gown, just like the one they had drawn.

It seemed a little bit magic that you could draw a dress on a piece of paper, and someone could make it real for you. Almost like having a fairy godmother. Even if *this* fairy godmother was a little bit slow!

'That might feel like a long time,' Katya said, as though reading Lola's mind, 'but to make a special dress like this, I have to first create a pattern, then cut it out, then sew it all together.'

As she spoke, Katya pointed past Headless to a large work table with scissors and brown cardboard and a sewing machine. That type of magic looked like a lot of hard work.

'But I promise you, Lola,' Katya said kindly, 'the next time you come in you'll be able to get an idea of how pretty you're going to look. Now, I'm just going to pop out the back again to get my notebook.'

As Katya left the room, Lola lifted the fabric and watched how it sort of floated down to the work table.

'I can't believe it's actually going to happen, Mum,' she squealed.

'Me neither,' her mum laughed back, giving Lola a huge squeeze. 'It's like a dream come true!'

Chapter Two

As Lola hugged her mum, she thought back to the moment she'd first found out.

Lola and Will had just come back from their karate class. She had been *starving* and the smell of a roast dinner in the oven was almost too much to bear. Lola's mum, Helen, was humming a tune in the kitchen while Rex chopped up some beans.

As soon as her mum walked into the lounge room, Lola knew something was up. Her mum was smiling, and the way she kept looking at Rex was different, somehow.

'Guys. Sit down. We've got some news,' she said.

Lola sneaked a look at Will. He was doing his eyebrow thing. Will always raised his eyebrows when he was wondering about something. When he and Rex had first moved in, it used to annoy Lola. Now she was used to it and even kind of liked it.

Lola sat next to Will and his raised eyebrows.

'Well,' Rex began in a very serious voice, 'you know that Helen and I love each other very much.'

'Daaad,' Will groaned.

Rex chuckled. 'Sorry, mate,' he said, ruffling Will's hair. 'The thing is ...'

He smiled at Lola's mum and his voice trailed off.

'The thing is,' Lola's mum picked up, 'we've decided, well, as long as you kids are OK with it ...'

Lola threw her hands up in the air. 'What have you decided?' she asked. Really, for grown-ups, the two of them were acting kind of silly.

'We've decided ...' Rex said.

'To get married!' Lola's mum exclaimed.

'OK, Helen,' Katya said, sitting at the work table with her notebook ready. 'Did you get the measurements of the other flower girl? The one who lives interstate?'

'Yes,' Lola's mum said, fishing around in her handbag for a piece of paper. 'These are Tess's measurements.'

Lola scratched her head as Katya jotted the figures into her notebook. She had been so excited when her mum asked her to be a flower girl that she'd almost forgotten to breathe. She'd only ever been to one wedding before. It had been pretty cool. But *this* wedding was going to be the absolute coolest day of her entire life!

In fact, she'd been so excited about it that she'd almost forgotten there was going to be a *second* flower girl.

Tess was Will's cousin, and she was going to fly down with her family the week before the big wedding.

It was kind of weird to think that Will had cousins Lola hadn't even met. All Lola knew was that Tess was a few years younger than her, and that she had a brother who was going to be a paige boy with Will.

Lola grinned to herself. She knew lots of girls from school who were about Tess's age. Her favourite was a little girl who was blonde and cute and a bit shy. Sometimes, Lola and her friends let her join in their games at lunchtime.

Maybe Tess would be just like that?

'Thanks, Katya,' Lola's mum interrupted her thoughts. 'Hot chocolate time, Lola?'

Lola nodded, and thoughts about Tess flew out of her mind.

For the moment, anyway.

Chapter Three

Later that afternoon, Lola sat with her mum and her best friend Abbey in the lounge room. About a thousand magazines were strewn all over the coffee table. Will concentrated on tapping the buttons of his Game Boy. The tapping sound ran around the room.

Abbey pushed her hair back and let out a massive sigh.

'You are the luckiest duck in the universe, Loles!' she said. 'I wish *my* mum and dad would get married.'

'But they're already married,' Lola's mum reminded her.

'Then I wish they'd get married *again,*' Abbey giggled.

Lola's mum laughed. 'Well,' she said, 'the wedding will be fun. But there's a lot to organise. I definitely need a cup of tea before I continue.'

'Yes please,' Lola and Abbey said together.

'Waiter, can I have a glass of milk?' Will added cheekily, continuing his Game Boy *tap, tap, tap*.

Lola's mum rolled her eyes. 'OK Loles, while I'm gone, maybe you can have a look at some flowers for you and Tess. Perhaps you could come up with some ideas of what might go with your purple dresses.'

As soon as Lola's mum had left the room, Abbey started acting crazy. 'Look what I found,' she whispered.

Lola stared as Abbey pulled out a brochure that was tucked away in the back of a bridal magazine. She noticed the title first. 'Hawaiian Honeymoon Bliss' was written in big, bold letters across the top of the brochure. Underneath the words, there was a picture of a lovely beach with golden sands and bright blue water.

Abbey pointed to it about a hundred times. Then she flipped the brochure over to the back page.

Written in black texta in her mum's handwriting were two dates. Lola noticed that the first date was the day after the wedding.

Lola could already imagine swimming in the clear water with Will, building huge sandcastles, eating cold ice-creams ...

'Awesome!' she exclaimed loudly. 'We're going to Hawaii!'

Will paused from tapping his Game Boy and leant over to look at the brochure.

'Loles,' he said slowly, 'it's a *honeymoon*. Dad and your mum are going. Not us.

That's why Aunty Kay is coming with Beau and Tess. So she can look after us.'

I want to go on holiday!

Lola watched as her mum came back into the lounge room with the tray of drinks. She kept watching her mum as she sneaked two spoonfuls of sugar in her tea.

'So, what do you think of these flowers, Loles?' her mum asked, pointing at a picture.

Lola breathed in. The flowers were *perfect*. Some of them were light pink, and others were purple. They were tied with a green bow that looked great with the green leaves.

But, right now, she couldn't stop thinking about what Will had said.

'Mum,' she said slowly, 'is it true? Are you and Rex going on a honeymoon without us?' Lola reached for a third spoonful of sugar as she spoke. Normally her mum wouldn't let her have three whole spoonfuls in her tea. But she didn't say anything about it this time.

'Oh, sweetie,' Lola's mum said. 'I'm sorry. It's just been so crazy lately. I thought

I told you that Will's Aunty Kay was coming with Beau and Tess to look after you while Rex and I go on our honeymoon.'

Mum's going away without me!

Lola reached for a fourth spoonful of sugar, but this time her mum pushed the bowl away.

'Loles, Rex and I are going away together. We haven't had much time to be on our own, and it's only for a week ...'

'I'll be here,' Abbey said brightly. 'And you're going to have a brand new *girl* cousin in the house. Which is pretty lucky, because I'll just be stuck with Dumb and Dumber, as usual!'

Lola felt a little smile twitching around her lips. Dumb and Dumber were Abbey's not-so-nice pet names for her brothers.

Lola drew a circle around the perfect flowers in the brochure. Then she let the twitch turn into a smile. Lola had the wedding to look forward to. And she was going to have a little girl in her house for once.

Abbey was right. She *was* the luckiest duck in the entire universe!

Chapter Four

Lola counted down the days until Will's cousins arrived. Five sleeps seemed like a very long time. But finally, she stood with her family in the Arrivals section of the airport. It was fascinating watching everyone come through the sliding doors. Some people waved and laughed as they were met by friends and family. Some cried and hugged.

'Is that them, Rex?' Lola asked for the hundredth time, jiggling her hand impatiently in his.

'No. No … yes!' Rex said finally. 'That's them now! Just coming out of the door.'

'Beau!' Will yelled. 'Over here!'

Lola stayed close to her mum and Rex. It was a bit strange to see Aunty Kay. She looked a lot like Rex but with long hair.

Lola felt herself staring as Beau waved at Will. She'd thought that Beau would be younger than Will, since Tess was younger than her. But he actually looked about Will's age. He was wearing really baggy pants and a baseball cap that sat backwards on his head.

Then Lola looked down.

The little girl who sort of *bounced* towards them was nothing like Lola had imagined. Tess was small and thin. Her hair was jet black, and cut into a jagged bob that bounced up and down as she jogged over to them.

'Hi, Uncle Rex!' she squealed, leaping into Rex's arms so that he had to let go of Lola's hand to catch her. 'I got a colouring book on the plane! And a box of pencils! And two biscuits in little packets, but I saved one of them!'

'Did you, sweetheart?' Rex said, putting Tess on his hip while he kissed Aunty Kay and gave Beau a handshake. 'Kay, this is

Helen, and this is Lola,' he introduced. 'My girls,' he added proudly.

'It's lovely to meet you,' Aunty Kay said, giving Lola's mum a hug and then turning to Lola. 'And you too, Lola,' she said. As soon as Aunty Kay smiled, Lola liked her. Her smile was just like Rex's.

Lola watched as Tess grabbed Rex's cheeks, pulling his attention back to her.

'You know why I saved one of the biscuits, Uncle Rex?' she asked, squishing his cheeks together. Rex's smile was square between her small hands.

Lola watched as Tess jumped out of Rex's arms and landed beside her. In two seconds, there was a crumbling biscuit being pressed into her hand.

'I saved it for my new cousin!' Tess announced loudly, making sure that *everyone* was watching her. 'Lola!'

At bedtime, Lola stepped over Tess's suitcase and around the edges of the trundle bed where Tess lay. Lola's bedroom had never seemed quite so small before. Of course, she'd had people stay over. But somehow, even though Tess was tiny, she seemed to take up a lot of space.

She could hear Beau and Will talking and laughing in Will's room next door.

The boys had been playing together all day. Which had left Lola with Tess ...

'Lola?' Tess said, sitting up in her bed. 'What's your favourite colour?'

Lola got into bed and yawned. She felt like she'd been asked more questions in one day than in her entire life put together.

'Ah, purple,' she said.

'Me too!' Tess said enthusiastically.

Lola snuggled under the doona and closed her eyes.

'Lola?' Tess's voice ripped into her almost-sleep. 'Which do you like better, big dogs or little dogs?'

It was hard to roll her eyes while they were closed.

'Little dogs,' Lola said, letting the words drift out on another yawn.

Suddenly, Lola felt her arm being yanked. She opened her eyes.

'Me too!' Tess exclaimed. 'Because you can pick them up and cuddle them.'

Lola tugged her arm back.

'Night, Tess,' she said hopefully.

'Night, Lola,' Tess replied.

Lola rolled over and let the waves of sleep wash over her. It had been a long day, and it was a gorgeous feeling to let go and drift into a deep sleep. Down, down …

'Lola?'

Tess's voice woke her up with a jolt.

'What's your favourite animal?'

Chapter Five

'Lola, let's see whose legs are longer. Straighten yours out,' said Tess.

She and Tess were stuck in the tiny back seats of Rex's car, facing the back window.

It was time for the second dress fitting, and *everyone* was coming. Will and Beau were getting their suits from a shop a few doors down from the dressmaker's.

Rex was driving and Lola's mum sat in the front. Will and Beau sat in the middle seats with Aunty Kay. And Lola and Tess were …

'Lola!', Tess said, nudging her, '*straighten your legs out.*'

'We're here, guys,' Rex called from the driver's seat.

When he opened the door, Lola was glad to get out.

'You girls are divine!' Lola's mum exclaimed. 'Just take a look at yourselves.'

Lola stood on Katya's little stool,

with Tess on the ground in front of her. She looked down at her purple dress. Lola could feel the fabric over her shoulders. She loved the way the skirt flared at the bottom. It was really gorgeous!

She hopped off the stool and turned to look in the mirror. All she could see was her own head and a purple Tess spinning around to make herself dizzy.

'You look really pretty, Tess,' Lola said. 'Like a little princess.'

Lola's mum rubbed Lola's back in little circles. It was the sort of touch that said 'well done'. It was the sort of touch that made Lola want to lean in and give her mum a big cuddle. A cuddle that would say how much Lola would miss her when she went away on her honeymoon.

But before she was able to step close enough, Tess jumped in between them.

'Actually, I look like a *big* princess,' Tess corrected.

Lola frowned as she looked over Tess's head at her mum. She screwed up her face to show how annoying Tess was. Her mum gave her a half-smile. Lola knew that face. It was asking her to be patient. Lola took a deep breath.

The purple fabric made a lovely swishing sound around Lola's knees as she walked past Tess towards the mirror.

'Do you mind if I take a look too,

big princess?' said Lola.

Lola stood beside Tess in front of the mirror. Their reflections stared back.

'We look exactly the same!' Tess declared happily.

'So, Mum,' Lola said, lifting her hair up with her hands, 'do you think I could have an 'up' hairstyle like this?'

Tess copied her hand movements, lifting her black bob in the same way.

'Or do you think it might be better to do this?' Lola continued, holding her hair up in two pigtails. Next to her, Tess copied the second hairstyle – only one of her pigtails was very high, and the other was very low.

When Lola swung around to look at her mum, Tess swung around too. It almost felt like she had a small, colourful shadow, especially when Lola crossed her arms and the colourful shadow crossed hers. But this shadow had a very loud voice!

'Hey, look,' Tess called suddenly. 'Beau and Will are making silly window-squish faces.'

Lola turned to the shop window. Beau and Will were standing out the front of the shop. They were wearing black suits with little black bow ties. Even with their faces squished to the window pane, they still looked really cool.

Lola felt a little pang as she watched

Beau and Will crack up laughing and run away. The two of them were like best friends. Which wasn't the same thing as having a talkative shadow…

'Come on, girls,' Aunty Kay interrupted Lola's thoughts. 'It's shoe time!'

Lola had never been into such a beautiful shoe shop.

There were pink shoes with butterfly clips on the front. And red shoes that looked like they might belong to Dorothy out of *The Wizard of Oz*. There were white shoes made from shiny satin.

And, best of all, there were silver, sparkly shoes with a heel and little bows at the front.

Lola could hardly breathe as she picked them up. 'Mum?' she said, holding the shoes out. 'Pleeease?'

Lola's mum looked doubtful. 'They are lovely, Loles,' she said, 'but I think the heels are a little bit high. I'm not sure they would be very comfortable.' She gave Lola a funny look, with her head tilting towards Tess. 'You know ... for *both* of you,' she added in a whisper.

'Then maybe Tess can get *these* ones,' Lola suggested, picking up a pair of silver ballet flats. They were quite similar to the ones she liked, except for the heels.

'Nuh-uh!' Tess declared. 'I want to have exactly the same shoes as Lola!'

Tess's expression reminded Lola of a storm cloud. All dark and brooding and ready to rain. 'Absolutely *exactly* the same,' she added, just to make sure everyone understood her.

'Look, sweetie,' Lola's mum said, 'I think we'll go with the ballet flats. They'll be better for *everyone*. It's a good compromise.'

Lola reluctantly put the shoes with a heel back on the shelf. If it wasn't for Tess, she was pretty sure that her mum would have let her have them.

Honestly, it's not fair, Lola thought as her mum paid for the two pairs of ballet flats.

Lola walked quickly back to the car, hoping to lose Tess for a moment. But the shadow just ran to keep up with her.

As Lola tucked herself into the tiny back seat, she turned around and saw Beau and Will laughing and chatting in the middle row.

She knew what her mum meant by the word *compromise*. Compromising was when people changed what they wanted a little bit so it would suit everyone.

Lola crossed her arms and stared out the back window, ignoring Tess's chatter.

Why am I the only one who has to compromise?

Chapter Six

The next morning, Lola got up very quietly so as not to wake Tess. She pulled on her green tracksuit pants and a grey T-shirt and went for a walk around the block.

When she got back, Rex was in the kitchen making bacon and eggs. 'Scrambled, poached or fried?' Rex asked.

'Poached, please,' Lola said.

'Me too,' came Tess's voice. 'And where did you go without me?'

Lola looked around. Tess was dressed in jeans and a shirt. Before Lola could answer, Tess had disappeared in the direction of Lola's bedroom.

'Did you have a nice walk, Loles?' Rex asked, cracking eggs into some boiling water in a saucepan.

'Yes, thanks,' she said. 'Freddie the dog barked at me. I think he wanted to come for a walk.' Freddie lived a few doors down from Lola's house. 'So I just gave him a pat through the fence,' Lola continued.

Lola was going to keep talking, but Tess interrupted.

'We're going to visit Uncle Phil today. And stay the night,' Tess said.

Lola turned around. Tess had changed. Instead of jeans and a shirt, she was now wearing tracksuit pants and a T-shirt. And a giant smile.

'See, Loles?' she said. 'We're practically *exactly* the same again. Don't we both look cool?'

Tess is copying me again!

Rex gave Lola a wink as he put a plate of poached eggs in front of her. It was as though he thought it was funny.

Lola put her head between her hands. In a way, it *was* kind of funny that Tess was trying to look like her. And she had to admit that Tess looked pretty cute.

But another part of her just felt *over* it all! The constant questions were one thing. Lola could *almost* handle that. And she was *almost* getting used to Tess following her around everywhere.

Honestly though, Tess wasn't just a shadow ... She was a real copycat.

'Hey Lola, do you want to play soccer?' Will asked later that day.

Will kicked the ball from foot to foot as he spoke. Then he kicked it up to his head and butted it towards the mantelpiece.

'Yep,' Lola replied, butting it back towards him before it could do any damage.

It felt good to be walking to the park with Will. Just the two of them for once. Since Beau and Tess had arrived, she had hardly played with Will at all.

Lola wasn't sure it was very nice of her, but she had to admit she was glad that Tess and the others had gone to stay with Uncle Phil for the night.

'Now, I'll show you a trick that Beau taught me,' Will said as they arrived at the park.

Lola watched as Will kicked the ball upwards. As it rose, he leant forward. The ball rested behind his head, on the back of his shoulders. When he straightened up, he moved back very quickly, and it dropped down to his feet again.

'That is *seriously* cool!' Lola said.

'I know!' Will grinned. 'It's great hanging out with Beau. He's taught me heaps of stuff like that.'

Lola felt that strange, annoyed feeling rise through her. It wasn't something she could talk to Will about.

But the more she thought about it, the more unfair it seemed that Will got to hang out with someone his own age. Someone who could actually teach him stuff. Especially when Lola was stuck answering a gazillion questions!

'Wanna have a go?' Will asked, breaking into her thoughts.

Lola nodded. She wasn't going to let a silly feeling ruin time with Will on the soccer field.

'OK. Kick up. Now lean forward … oh *almost*, Loles!' said Will. 'Kick up, lean forward …'

Will was being really encouraging. Even when she caught the ball on her

head instead of her back, he kept on trying to teach her.

When Lola finished the trick properly for the first time, Will screamed and punched the air.

'You did it! You're a *legend,* Lola,' he said.

Lola grinned. She was happy that Rex and her mum were getting married. She was happy that Will was going to be her brother.

Even if she did have to put up with copycat Tess.

Chapter Seven

Lola put a bookmark in her book and laid it on her bedside table. She wriggled around under her doona to make her bed extra warm. Then she looked at her clock.

It was ten minutes past her normal bedtime, and her mum *still* hadn't come in for a goodnight kiss.

Finally, Lola heard her mum's footsteps down the hall.

'Hey, sweetie,' she said, coming in and sitting on Lola's bed. 'I've been trying to write some vows for the wedding ceremony. Rex has already written his, and he won't show me. It's really hard to come up with something special. Something that suits us and our family.'

Lola nodded. 'You'll think of something, Mum,' she said.

Lola's mum lifted up the doona and snuggled in next to Lola.

'And what about you, Loles? What have you been up to this afternoon?'

Lola loved this part of the day. The bit where she had her mum all to herself.

First, she told her mum about Will

teaching her the soccer trick at the park. She thrashed around under the doona, trying to demonstrate without getting out of bed.

'So, Beau taught Will the trick. And then Will taught me, and it took ages but I finally got it,' Lola explained.

Lola's mum pushed Lola's hair behind her ears. 'It's really nice, having them stay, isn't it?' she said. 'We're lucky they can look after you while Rex and I are away.'

Suddenly, Lola felt cross again. 'Why can't we come to Hawaii?' she asked. 'I don't want to stay here with Tess for a whole week.'

Before she knew it, Lola was blurting everything out. She hadn't had her mum to herself for days and it felt like there was a whole build-up of feelings that just wanted to rush out of her mouth.

'Mum, Tess copies just about *everything* I do. If I want poached eggs, she wants poached eggs. If I wear my tracksuit pants, she changes into her tracksuit pants. If I say my favourite colour is purple, she says her favourite colour is purple. And she asks more questions than ... well, more questions than any other person on this planet. And she won't leave me alone. It's driving me nuts!'

'Hmm, I've noticed that Tess copies you a bit,' her mum said with a nod. 'But it's only because she admires you, Loles.

She wants to be just like you. Which, if you think about it, is kind of sweet. I guess you'll just have to be patient with her.'

'Patient?' Lola repeated. 'How come *I* have to be patient? Will doesn't have to be! He just gets to have fun with Beau.'

Lola's mum had a knowing look on her face. 'So, Will wasn't patient this afternoon when he taught you the soccer trick?' she said slowly.

Lola shrugged. She had to admit that there was at least a little bit of truth in what her mum was saying. Perhaps she *could* try to be a bit more patient with Tess.

Really, part of her enjoyed the way Tess copied her. It *was* kind of flattering.

And Tess *was* kind of cute, even with all her annoying ways.

But as her mum stroked her hair, Lola realised that there was something else making her anxious. She felt a tear trickle down her cheek. She'd never been away from her mum for a whole week before ...

'Mum,' she whispered, 'I'm going to miss you so much when you go on your honeymoon. I wish you guys were taking me and Will.'

Lola's mum pulled her close. Her hug was tight and warm. 'Loles, I love you more than the earth and the stars. I love Will, too. And Rex loves both of you. Even when we're not with you, we are still thinking about you. We don't have to be together all the time to be ... *together*,' she finished.

Lola breathed into her mum's chest. Suddenly she felt a tickle on her tummy.

'Where do you live?' her mum asked.

Lola felt a giggle brewing inside her. It wasn't just because of the tickle. It was also because she knew the game her mum was starting up. It was a game they'd played for as long as Lola could remember.

'Ryrie Court,' Lola played along.

'And where else do you live?' Lola's mum egged her on.

Lola struggled to keep her face straight. 'In my home. With my family.'

'And where else do you live?' Lola's mum asked with an extra ticklish tickle.

Lola let her answer out with a squeal and a laugh. 'In your HEART!'

Chapter Eight

Lola closed her eyes as a little puff of hairspray travelled towards her pigtails.

It was great fun to be sitting at the hairdresser's with her mum and Aunty Kay and Tess in a long row. Lola uncrossed her legs and leant closer to the mirror. Beside her, she could see Tess also uncrossing her legs, and looking in the mirror.

'What do you think of Lola's hair, Helen?' the hairdresser asked, spinning Lola's stool towards her.

'I think it's perfect,' Lola's mum said. 'I think *you're* perfect, Lola,' she added in a whisper.

'Especially with the tracksuit pants,' Lola said with a grin. Even though everyone's hair was done now, they still hadn't put on their wedding outfits. Lola couldn't *wait* for that moment.

'Mum, I can't believe we're actually, honestly, truly getting married today!' She giggled before she corrected herself, 'I mean, that *you and Rex* are getting married today.'

Lola's mum gave her a wink. She looked really pretty. Her hair was up in a loose bun, and wispy bits fell over her face. She looked back in the mirror, but she was looking at Lola, not at herself.

Suddenly, Tess scrambled up onto Lola's lap, and all Lola could see in the mirror was Tess's pigtailed head.

'Hey, Lola!' she said. 'We're allowed to wear some lip gloss!'

Back at home, Lola reached out a finger to fix up Tess's lip gloss. There seemed to be more on Tess's chin than on her lips.

Lola tapped her foot on the lounge room carpet. Her mum and Aunty Kay had been in the bedroom for *ages*.

'Loles, can you draw me a big wedding cake?' Tess asked.

Lola stared at the stack of paper on the coffee table. So far, she'd drawn a tiny cake, a medium sized cake, and a hundred flower girls, big and small.

She picked up her pencil, but just then she heard the bedroom door open.

As Aunty Kay and Lola's mum entered the lounge room, Lola's eyes grew wide. Her mouth seemed stuck in the shape of an 'O'.

Lola had always thought her mum was

pretty. But the lady in front of her was *beautiful!* The sky-blue dress had a heart-shaped neckline, with no straps. It came in at her mum's waist, and flowed down to the floor. And peeping out from under her mum's dress were a pair of dark blue shoes with diamanté buckles.

Wow, you look beautiful!

Lola let her eyes wander back up to her mum's face. Her cheeks were brushed lightly with rouge, and her eyelashes looked longer and darker than normal. With her hair up and wispy, she looked …

'Mum …' Lola breathed, 'you look, you look …'

'Like a princess. A *big* princess!' Tess finished for her.

They all cracked up laughing.

Lola almost wished the day could be frozen right here, right now.

Four girls. Laughing. In the lounge room. With a wedding ahead of them.

Lola had never been in a limousine before. For a moment, she pictured Will's reaction. He totally loved cars, and he would have loved to be travelling with Rex and Beau in a car that had been s-t-r-e-t-c-h-e-d like this.

The boys had got ready at Uncle Phil's house, so that Rex wouldn't see Lola's mum in her wedding gown. Apparently that was bad luck. But Lola knew in her heart that *nothing* could go wrong today!

The driver wore a suit with gold buttons and a cap with gold trim. When he opened the door for them, Lola couldn't help giggling.

She slid onto one of the bench seats. Tess got in next to her, and her mum and

Aunty Kay sat facing them. It felt more like a fancy room on wheels than a car.

'Are you ready, Helen?' Aunty Kay asked as the driver pulled away from the curb.

Lola noticed her mum gulp. She smoothed down her blue dress. She looked out the window and then back at Kay.

'I'm a bit nervous,' she admitted. 'You know, having to say wedding vows in front of everyone.'

'I know what a vow is,' Tess said knowingly. 'A vow is like a promise.'

Lola crossed her legs. She put her bouquet on the seat between her and Tess. Tess crossed her legs. Then she put her bouquet right on top of Lola's.

'I think there will be a *hundred* people watching us when we get out of this car, or perhaps even *fifty*,' Tess added happily.

Lola glanced at her mum. She tried to think of something to say to help her feel less nervous. But suddenly the limousine pulled to a halt.

'Ladies. We have arrived,' the driver said, tipping his cap.

Chapter Nine

It was perfect weather for a wedding in the park. The sun was shining but it wasn't too hot.

The wedding guests stood, all dressed up, in two groups with an aisle down the middle. At the end of the aisle, a white gazebo just like the one in *The Sound of Music* was decorated with flowers and bows.

Standing in the gazebo were Rex, Will and Beau. They turned and watched as the girls came down the path.

Lola thought it was funny to see Will standing so still. Normally he was jumping around and fidgeting. But now he looked very serious.

Lola and Tess walked slowly down the aisle, smiling and waving at people as they went past. Lola's mum walked behind them, holding her giant bouquet.

Lola had thought walking down the aisle might be a bit scary. But she knew heaps of the people there. She grinned as Uncle Phil blew her a kiss with both hands, and then did a funny bow. Her grandma smiled and Abbey waved to her. And she could *feel* everyone's happiness. It wasn't scary at all. It was fun!

When they got to the gazebo, Lola stood between her mum and Tess. Lola's mum and Rex held hands.

'Ladies and gentlemen,' said the wedding celebrant who stood in front of them on a little platform. 'We are gathered here today to celebrate the union of Rex and Helen.'

Lola glanced around. The guests were standing all around the gazebo now, in a semi-circle. Lola twirled her bouquet until it was time for Rex to say his vows.

'I promise,' he began. Lola noticed

that Rex had to clear his throat and start again.

'I promise to love and honour the beautiful Helen. I promise to respect her.' He looked at Lola before he continued. 'And to care for the lovely daughter I've always wanted ...'

Lola felt her cheeks redden, but it was a nice kind of embarrassment.

'Hey, what about me?' Will interrupted from next to Rex.

The guests all laughed. Rex smiled. 'And you too, if you behave,' he added.

It took a while for the laughter to die down. Lola smiled but she couldn't quite relax. Part of her was worried for her mum.

Lola hoped that she had been able to think up some wedding vows of her own.

Lola gulped as her beautiful mum opened her mouth and closed it again. Then Rex cupped his hands around her mum's, and this seemed to help.

'I promise to love and honour Rex,' Lola's mum said slowly and clearly. The guests were completely silent. 'I promise to cherish our beautiful family.

'And I promise that each of you will be right with me, always, even when we're not together.' Lola's mum looked across at Will. Then at Rex. Then her eyes landed on Lola and stayed there.

Lola pushed her lips together so she wouldn't cry. She knew what her mum was going to say next.

'Because you all live right here,' Helen said, clutching the bouquet against her chest, 'in my heart.'

Chapter Ten

Lola sat at the kids' table at the wedding reception. Her feet bumped against her empty rose-petal basket. It had been fun throwing the petals over her mum and Rex. She and Tess had giggled all the way through the photo session too. When the photographer had told them to say 'cheese', Lola knew that was supposed to help them smile. But they hadn't needed any help at all. Lola's face ached from all the smiles. Real smiles.

'Hey Lola, let's go and get thirds,' Tess said, popping the last piece of wedding cake on her plate into her mouth.

Lola groaned and shook her head. 'I think I'm full, Tess,' she said.

'But you can *never* be full of chocolate cake with pink icing!' Tess protested. 'All right then, let's just get more punch,' she added, giving Lola a little punch on the arm.

Lola smiled and followed Tess to the drinks' table. She looked around the reception centre. Some of the guests had swapped tables to chat with other friends. Others stood around, clinking glasses, chatting and laughing.

Lola looked at the band, which was warming up on the stage at the front of the room. Then she used the ladle to serve herself and Tess glasses of punch.

As the girls walked back to their table, the band started playing.

Lola watched as Rex took her mum's hand and they walked to the dance floor.

Lola knew that the dance they were doing was called a 'waltz'. She loved the way her mum's dress swished around as she moved. She loved the way Rex held her around the waist and dipped her down.

She watched as he lifted her mum back to standing position.

Soon, heaps of the guests had joined them. Lola giggled as she spotted Will twirling on the dance floor with Aunty Kay and raising his eyebrows again.

'Lola?' Tess said, tugging at her arm. 'Lola?'

Lola looked back at Tess. Tess had a worried expression as she pushed her chair back from the table and glanced down at her feet.

'I'm sorry about the shoes,' she said. 'I'm sorry I made you get the same ones as me. I know you really wanted the other ones. I hope you like them, just a little bit?'

Lola gave Tess a special smile. She put her feet next to Tess's in a line. 'I *love* the shoes, Tess,' she said. 'And I reckon they're *dancing* shoes! Should we try them?'

Lola loved how Tess's face lit up. Her grin ran from ear to ear.

As they walked towards the dance floor, Tess grabbed Lola's hand. She pulled Lola down towards her so she could whisper in her ear. 'You are the bestest cousin in the whole, entire universe,' she said to Lola. 'You're a *legend*.'

Lola squeezed Tess's hand. She thought about how Will had taught her the soccer trick, and then told her she was a legend. Maybe Will found *her* annoying sometimes.

But then again, maybe that was all part of being family.

As she pulled Tess onto the dance floor, Lola leant down and whispered in her ear. '*You're* the bestest too, Tess,' she said. '*You are a legend.*'

Lola blinked sleepily and looked up at her bedside table. Her rose-petal basket was no longer empty – it was now full of tiny chocolates that she and Tess had collected from all the tables after they'd exhausted themselves dancing.

At the end of the wedding she had fallen

asleep on two chairs pushed together. Tess and Will and Beau had done the same on some chairs opposite.

Lola had woken up when Rex carried her to the car, but she'd pretended she was still asleep.

Later that night, Lola woke up for a moment and was glad to hear Tess's breathing on the trundle bed next to her.

Lola knew she would be in her mum's heart while her mum was in Hawaii. She hoped her mum and Rex would have the best time ever.

Because Lola knew she was going to have a great time, right here, at home. Even if she *did* miss her mum and Rex, it was pretty amazing that she had Will and Beau and Aunty Kay, and even Tess, to look after her.

And they were family too.